W9-AHW-847

Dear Parent:

Congratulations! Your child is taking the first steps on an exciting journey. The destination? Independent reading!

STEP INTO READING® will help your child get there. The program offers five steps to reading success. Each step includes fun stories and colorful art. There are also Step into Reading Sticker Books, Step into Reading Math Readers, Step into Reading Write-In Readers, Step into Reading Phonics Readers, and Step into Reading Phonics First Steps! Boxed Sets—a complete literacy program with something for every child.

Learning to Read, Step by Step!

Ready to Read Preschool–Kindergarten
• **big type and easy words** • **rhyme and rhythm** • **picture clues**
For children who know the alphabet and are eager to begin reading.

Reading with Help Preschool–Grade 1
• **basic vocabulary** • **short sentences** • **simple stories**
For children who recognize familiar words and sound out new words with help.

Reading on Your Own Grades 1–3
• **engaging characters** • **easy-to-follow plots** • **popular topics**
For children who are ready to read on their own.

Reading Paragraphs Grades 2–3
• **challenging vocabulary** • **short paragraphs** • **exciting stories**
For newly independent readers who read simple sentences with confidence.

Ready for Chapters Grades 2–4
• **chapters** • **longer paragraphs** • **full-color art**
For children who want to take the plunge into chapter books but still like colorful pictures.

STEP INTO READING® is designed to give every child a successful reading experience. The grade levels are only guides. Children can progress through the steps at their own speed, developing confidence in their reading, no matter what their grade.

Remember, a lifetime love of reading starts with a single step!

BARBIE and associated trademarks and trade dress are owned by, and used under license from, Mattel, Inc. © 2005 Mattel, Inc. All Rights Reserved.
Published in the United States by Random House Children's Books, a division of Random House, Inc., New York, and in Canada by Random House of Canada Limited, Toronto.
No part of this book may be reproduced or copied in any form without permission from the copyright owner.

STEP INTO READING, RANDOM HOUSE, and the Random House colophon are registered trademarks of Random House, Inc.

4871 4751 6/12

www.stepintoreading.com
www.barbie.com

Educators and librarians, for a variety of teaching tools, visit us at
www.randomhouse.com/teachers

Library of Congress Cataloging-in-Publication Data
Jordan, Apple.
On your toes / by Apple Jordan ; illustrated by Karen Wolcott.
    p.   cm. — (Step into reading. Step 1) "Barbie."
SUMMARY: Barbie and Kelly look at photographs of Barbie's ballet performances.
ISBN 978-0-375-83142-3 (trade) — ISBN 978-0-375-93142-0 (lib. bdg.)
[1. Ballet—Fiction.   2. Photographs—Fiction.   3. Dolls—Fiction.]
I. Wolcott, Karen, ill. II. Title. III. Series. PZ7.J755On 2005 [E]—dc22 2004005599

Printed in the United States of America   25 24 23 22 21 20 19 18 17 16

STEP INTO READING®

STEP 1

Barbie™
On Your Toes

by Apple Jordan

illustrated by Karen Wolcott

WITHDRAWN

Random House 🏠 New York

Barbie loves to dance!

She loves to leap.

She loves to jump.

She loves to spin.

And she loves
all the costumes!

"Do you like one best?"
Kelly asks.

Barbie is not sure.

She opens her album. . . .

Barbie is a princess.

She wears a pink tutu.

Her prince wakes her
with a kiss!

Barbie is a good swan.

She wears a white gown.

She is a bad swan, too.

She wears all black.

Barbie is a fairy
with a golden crown.

She dances with candy
canes and cookies.

21

Barbie is a magic bird.

She flies and flutters
on her toes.

Barbie is a puppet
who comes to life.

She bends and moves
as if she is on strings.

"I love all my costumes," says Barbie.

"But I love to dance
no matter what I wear!"

"Me too!" says Kelly.